Frances H. Edgar Rice

Biographical Sketch Of Timothy Bloomfield Edgar And His Wife

Frances H. Edgar Rice

Biographical Sketch Of Timothy Bloomfield Edgar And His Wife

ISBN/EAN: 9783741134388

Manufactured in Europe, USA, Canada, Australia, Japa

Cover: Foto ©Raphael Reischuk / pixelio.de

Manufactured and distributed by brebook publishing software
(www.brebook.com)

Frances H. Edgar Rice

Biographical Sketch Of Timothy Bloomfield Edgar And His Wife

BIOGRAPHICAL SKETCHES

OF

TIMOTHY BLOOMFIELD EDGAR

AND HIS WIFE,

MARY ANN BOYCE EDGAR.

WITH AN APPENDIX.

———

BY THEIR DAUGHTER,

FRANCES H. EDGAR RICE.

BY

FRANCES H. EDGAR RICE.

TO MY DEAR BROTHERS AND SISTERS

THESE SKETCHES
OF
OUR BELOVED PARENTS
ARE
AFFECTIONATELY DEDICATED.

" The record of the life of Timothy Bloomfield Edgar is full of instruction to the youth of our land. It carries with it the lesson that the faithful and unflinching discharge of duty in every relation of life, produces in the end the flower of a noble manhood, as surely as the dew and sunshine of the summer bring forth the ripened fruit."—*L. U. Reavis, in "St. Louis, the Future Great City of the World; Biographical Edition."*

INTRODUCTION.

Is it because this year (1892), is the four-hundredth anniversary of the discovery of a vast continent, of a new world, that the inhabitants of the land, at this historic period, peer so intently into the dim past, scan old manuscripts, records, sear and yellow with age, and search, as never before, among the ruins of fallen dynasties, for the why's and wherefore's of existing circumstances, midst which they now find themselves? These existing circumstances constitute the elements of a new and unique nation, and under such influences, at this period, an American cannot trace his own personal genealogy, without a blood-stirring realization that the building of the American Nation was no haphazard work, and the student of history soon perceives, that in the weaving of the web of the Nation's life, an all-seeing Eye penetrated the distant future, and that while fashioning and preparing the precious fabric, a powerful and unseen Hand guided and controlled the ever flitting shuttle. Such at least, is the thought vividly impressed upon the mind of the writer, as she traces the various and far-reaching ancestral lines of an American family, in which the elements that enter into the building of the American Nation are largely represented : amidst the throes and upheavings of the nations of the past, billows roll and toss, till at last, they break upon the shores of a new world ; and forth from the centuries that follow, emerge the typical American family, so well illustrated in these biographical sketches. For example, we see the transition of the Saxon family Edgar into that of a Scottish, in the story of the overthrow of the Saxon dynasty by the Norman Conquest. Again, a Norman family becomes an English one, according to the tradition of the Boyce family, which states that its members, natives of Neustria or Normandy, entered England with William the Conqueror ; in connection with the Boyce family, in the maternal line a Holland ancestry is introduced, while the Harrell family is Welsh-English, through a paternal ancestress (in a direct line) who was a sister of Sir Martin Frobisher [*] and whose maternal grandfather was a lord of York.[†] Thus in two persons, man and wife, standing at the head of an American family in 1892, we find the Saxon, Scottish, Norman, Welsh and English races represented, together with that of the Netherlands.

---

[*] According to his biographer (Frank Jones, B.A., London) Sir Martin Frobisher was held in high esteem by Queen Elizabeth, and that it was to his skill and bravery she largely attributed the great victory, won by the English, in the battle with the Spanish Armada.

[†] Father of Sir John York.

TIMOTHY BLOOMFIELD EDGAR.

"The prosperity of a country depends, not on the abundance of its revenues, nor on the strength of its fortifications, nor on the beauty of its public buildings; but it consists in the number of its cultivated citizens, in its men of education, enlightenment and character; here are to be found its true interest, its chief strength, its real power."—*Martin Luther.*

TIMOTHY BLOOMFIELD EDGAR was born at Rahway, New Jersey, January 20, 1815. He is a descendant (in the sixth generation) of David Edgar, of Keithock, male representative of Edgar of Wedderlie, Scotland. A son (Thomas) of this ancient House, a house with whose history, so much of romance and tragic story is associated, came to America and purchased an estate in New Jersey in 1725. The history of Mr. Edgar's maternal ancestry also abounds in romance, he being the fifth in descent from Edward Crowell, who arrived at Amboy, New Jersey, in 1705. The Crowell family (presumed to be descendants of Sir Henry Cromwell, grandfather of Oliver Cromwell, the Protector) holds a tradition, that two members of the family came to America in 1674, and that on the voyage to this continent they resolved to

7

change the name. With solemn ceremony this was done by writing the name of each on paper, each then cutting the letter " m " from the paper and casting it into the sea.* Interesting traditions concerning the patriotism of the Edgar, Crowell and Bloomfield families during the War of Independence also exist. According to the custom of the last century in large families — after acquiring such an education as the common schools afforded — sons who did not stay by the land, or had no land to till, who did not enter upon the professions or engage in maritime trade, were apprenticed to the trades. Accordingly, Alexander Edgar,† father of the subject of this sketch, was apprenticed to the trade of carpentry, and his son Timothy to that of coach-building. Before Mr. Edgar was of age, his employer, a distant relative, suggested that he go to New Orleans, and take charge of a branch house that had been established in that city. It had been the great desire of the youth's life to clear his father's

---

*" The family parchment or vellum recording these facts was in the possession of the Crowell family, in North Carolina, in an ornamental chest, with other valuables, when, by a party of 'Tarleton's Legion,' in 1781, the chest was seized and taken off. These facts are undoubted." -" Branches of the Crowell family removed from New Jersey to North Carolina and Virginia about 1722, and other members of the family continued to follow until the year 1740."—Edwin Salter, Washington, D. C., 1886. Sarah Crowell, wife of Alexander Edgar, and great-granddaughter of Edward Crowell, of Woodbridge, New Jersey, the founder of the family in America, also mentioned Cromwell as the original family name.—F. H. E. R.

† To Alexander Edgar and Sarah Crowell, his wife, were born nine children, seven sons and two daughters, of which family Timothy Bloomfield is the third son.

estate of an encumbrance ; this he had nearly accomplished, when a relative presented him with a clear title to the estate, before he departed on his long journey westward. Thus, the desire of his heart was gratified, ere he was twenty-one years of age. Mr. Edgar, on his way to New Orleans, passed through St. Louis, with which city he was greatly pleased. On his arrival, however, at his destination, he was not so favorably impressed, and decided to return to St. Louis and make it his future home. He left New Orleans in a sailing vessel, and arrived in New York City December, 1835, the memorable year of the great fire in that city. In April, 1836, Mr. Edgar came to St. Louis, Missouri, and established a carriage repository, at the corner of Fourth and Morgan streets. In the course of a few years, he purchased and improved the property at Nos. 409 and 411 North Third street. The first coaches ever built in Missouri were built at Mr. Edgar's repository, for Colonel Thomas L. Price, and were used on lines running from St. Louis to the farther West, where they well served the purpose of the ante-railroad period.

In 1837 Mr. Edgar was married to Miss Mary Ann Boyce, daughter of Mr. William H. Boyce, who became a resident of St. Louis in 1828, and was an enterprising and public spirited citizen during the early periods of this century. To Mr. and Mrs. Edgar were born eight children, Frances H. (Mrs. Edward P. Rice, of Chicago),

William B., Emma C. (Mrs. Oliver F. Garrison, of Missouri), Joseph A., Selwyn C., Clara R., Clara M. (Mrs·
Charles D. McLure, of St. Louis), and Robert H. Two
children, Joseph Alexander and Clara R., died in
infancy.

At an early period, Mr. Edgar was a member of the
Board of Directors of the Dollar Savings Institution, and
when that institution was merged into the Exchange Bank
of St. Louis, he, as one of its leading spirits, devoted to
the latter much time and attention. "From this period
dates Mr. Edgar's career as a banker, with which impor-
tant branch of commerce he was identified many years
and in which he has won the unqualified confidence and
esteem of his fellow-citizens."* Under the "National
Banking Act" he organized the Second National Bank of
St. Louis, Missouri, of which institution he was president
several years.

In 1860, Mr. Edgar withdrew almost entirely from commercial life ; in this respect, he unwittingly resembles a
class of English and Scottish gentlemen, who, after having acquired a modest fortune, retire from the active business world, preferring to devote the remaining years of
life to philanthropy and to various branches of mental
culture. Little did he realize at this time, that he would
so soon enter upon the most active period of his life, and

---

*The cited paragraphs which follow in this sketch are from "Saint
Louis, the Future Great City of the World. Biographical edition."

that his time and talents would be engaged in sustaining a nation amid the throes of a civil war.

Mr. Edgar, together with several members of his family, now contemplated spending a year abroad, visiting the British Isles and the continent of Europe, but the dark cloud of war appeared on the horizon of the country, and as it grew more and more threatening, and finally broke with all its lurid terror, not only over his country, but upon the city and state of his adoption, he bade farewell to all thoughts of pleasure or travel, and took his position quietly, yet with great firmness, among those who were ready to sustain the National Government in its hour of peril and great need. A little episode may not be out of place here, illustrating how quickly war may produce a reign of terror in a peaceful, law-abiding city. A gentleman, scarcely knowing what course to pursue, on learning that on a certain Sunday the city would be sacked by the German citizens, called at Mr. Edgar's residence and asked permission to bring his family beneath his (Mr. Edgar's) roof for protection, stating, that in case of rapine, he thought Mr. Edgar's house would certainly escape pillage, as his firmness in sustaining the National Government was widely known. Mr. Edgar quickly assented, but noticing that the gentleman was armed, added, on one condition ; i. e., that no arms be brought into the house ; "for," said Mr. Edgar, "I have lived under, and been protected by the Government of the United States all my

11

life, and I believe that the government is able and will protect me and mine." The gentleman in question withdrew his request, saying he could not think of laying aside his arms at such a crisis. The sequence proved there had been no foundation for the terrible rumor.

It was in 1861, not long after this episode, "that General John C. Frémont, Commandant of the Department of the West, made a request for eighty thousand dollars in gold, to pay for ordnance. Mr. Edgar maintained that it was not only the duty of private citizens, but of banking institutions also, to strengthen the power of the government, and through his influence the money was furnished. On account of some informality in the voucher given by General Frémont, and the great demands upon the treasury of the government, Mr. Edgar was obliged to go to Washington City and give his personal attention to the matter ; he succeeded in making an equitable settlement, receiving eighty thousand dollars in gold for General Frémont's voucher."

"During the Civil War Mr. Edgar applied himself by every means to relieve the burdens of our people ; he was one of a committee of two (Mr. George Partridge, of St Louis, also being one) appointed by the Merchants' Exchange of St. Louis, to proceed to Washington City, and endeavor to secure payment of the government vouchers that had accumulated in St. Louis. About fifteen million dollars of these vouchers were held in this city, and were at a discount of from eight to ten per cent, while the community was suffering from the lack of currency. It was a delicate and difficult mission, but it was brought to a successful issue, though there were many prejudices to overcome, both in the minds of Mr. Stanton, Secretary of War, and Mr. Chase, Secretary of the Treasury.

"After the allowance of the claims, certificates of indebtedness, payable in bonds, under an agreement to hold them a certain period, were issued. This stipulation in the settlement, was, however, soon withdrawn and the transaction completed." It was at the time of this mission, during a conference with Secretary of War Stanton, that Mr. Partridge placed his foot upon Mr. Edgar's, thus warning him that he (Mr. Partridge) thought Mr. Edgar was pressing the matter too far to insure final success. In this transaction, there was an opportunity for both gentlemen to add greatly to their private fortunes, but neither indulged the thought for a moment, their one desire being to strengthen the finances of the city.*

A committee, known as the War Relief Committee, was appointed by the Court of St. Louis County, to relieve the needs of soldiers' families, the families of those in

* Mr. Edgar and Mr. Partridge being the first to receive information of the payment of the government vouchers, had an opportunity to buy any amount of said vouchers at a large discount before the order was made public by the government. In fact, a strong banking house of one of our great Eastern cities approached them on this point, but to such a proposition they, of course, gave no heed.

active service, as well as of those who had fallen on the battle fields. Twenty citizens constituted this committee ; of this organization Mr. Edgar was president, and held the office until the close of the war. "He managed the large disbursements of this War Relief Fund * * with universal satisfaction and with a degree of accuracy that seemed impossible."

In 1863 Mr. Edgar was appointed by the Governor of the State of Missouri (Hamilton R. Gamble) a trustee, of the Missouri Institution for the Education of the Blind, to which institution he devoted much time and thought for many years.

In 1864 he was elected a member of the Board of Corporators of the Soldiers' Orphans' Home, of which board he was treasurer, until the purpose for which the Home was established was fulfilled, and there was no longer any need of an institution of this character. Mr. Edgar was also a member of the Board of Public Schools of St. Louis for several years, and, as a member of the Board of Trustees of the Public School Library Association, was greatly interested in establishing this library in the interest of the public schools of the city.

Mr. Edgar was one of the founders of the Missouri Historical Society, of which organization he is a life member. (This society was organized several years previous to its incorporation.)

For some years he was one of the leaders in the

St. Louis Provident Association, which was one of the best organized city charities in the United States at that period.

When peace and prosperity again reigned, and he was relieved of the great responsibilities and many cares induced by the war, Mr. Edgar yielded to his taste for travel — this taste having always been great, had made him familiar with his own country— and in 1865, accompanied by his wife, a daughter and a son, he made a tour of Europe, and returned greatly refreshed, ready to enter again upon the duties of a citizen.

"In 1867 he organized the Continental Bank under the name of the National Loan Bank of St. Louis, and became its president ; the construction given the national banking law, demanded the elimination of the word national, and the present name, Continental, was adopted. On his return from Europe, he became a director in the Missouri Pacific Railway, and in 1873-4 was president of that great corporation." During his connection with this Board, the Pacific Railway purchased the interest of the State of Missouri in said corporation. Mr. Edgar was one of the committee (Mr. George R. Taylor, Mr. James H. Lucas and Mr. James H. Harrison, of St. Louis, and perhaps one other, constituting the committee), that negotiated the bonds for this purchase, amounting to seven millions of dollars.

"As a promoter of manufacturing interests his efforts

have been highly advantageous to the welfare of the State, of which the Glendale Zinc Works, of South St. Louis, are an example," in which his sons and other members of the family are now largely interested.

In 1880 Mr. Edgar resigned the presidency of the Continental Bank of St. Louis, thus severing his active connection with the commercial world. "During an exceptionally long period of active life he has had what might be called an unbroken success. He has been the custodian of the moneys of individuals and of corporations to a very large amount, every dollar of which has been satisfactorily accounted for." Ever the quiet gentleman in his own home, he is now, at the ripe age of seventy-seven years, always to be found in his library, among his cherished books. To his mother, he was a faithful and dutiful son, and a solace to her in her long days of widowhood ; to two younger brothers and a still younger sister he was as a father. As a husband, thoughtful and considerate. Devoted to the welfare of his children to an extreme degree, the fatherhood of the subject of this sketch, may be illustrated in the experience of a daughter ; the relation which she bore to her earthly father, greatly assisted her, in her early youth, to understand the love of her Heavenly Father toward his children, and to lovingly claim the blessings, so freely promised in his Word. Though very domestic in his tastes, his home was the center of a large and generous hospitality for many years.

In his religious belief his views are similar to those of the Friends, of which sect his parents were devoted members. He was, however, a warm friend of Dr. T. M. Post, and was for several years a trustee of the Society of the First Congregational Church, St. Louis, of which church Dr. Post was for many years the pastor.

"All through his life Mr. Edgar has received the merited commendations and sincere respect of all who knew him or his deeds. Keenly sensitive to the rights and feelings of others, he performs the duties of each day with conscientious care; unambitious of mere popular regard, he has yet won the admiration of a people, who cannot but speak his name kindly and with warm encomiums upon virtues, that are unostentatious, and yet none the less apparent. Honors and success follow unsought in the path of such a life," but above and beyond all else, it bears the testimony, that he serves his generation in his day and that truly he liveth not unto himself.

CHAPTER II.

Blessed is the man that walketh not in the counsel of the ungodly,
Nor standeth in the way of sinners,
Nor sitteth in the seat of the scornful.
But his delight is in the law of the Lord;
And in his law doth he meditate day and night.
And he shall be like a tree planted by the rivers of water,
That bringeth forth its fruit in its season,
Whose leaf also shall not wither;
And whatsoever he doeth shall prosper.

— Psalms I. 1-3.

AMONG the colonial families of New Jersey, were found the ancestors of Mr. Edgar, and now, we have but to sail down the Atlantic Coast, as far as the State of North Carolina, where, on its sea-washed strands, in those counties, whose water courses are but the arteries of a great ocean threading the land, as, with fitful pulse, the stormy deep, throbs and surges through the Albemarle, we find the home of the ancestors of his wife, Mary Ann Boyce. In three counties; i. e., Bertie, Hertford and Gates, and perhaps in others lying near the sea, were located as planters, the various colonial families, from which sprang her ancestors. In these counties mentioned, early in the eighteenth century, are found the names of Gardiner and Harrell, families, from which

18

sprang ancestors in the direct maternal line ; in the paternal line, the name of Hardy appears at the same period, but that of Boyce, cannot be traced until later in the same century. This may be accounted for in various ways. First, the family seems to have been a small one, especially in its male representation ; second, old family records have become scattered and cannot be easily traced, since the male line, so far as known, has been extinct for a number of years. It scarcely can be doubted, however, that members of the family, came to this country during that early period, when excitement ran high, and the desire of nations to explore new lands and seas was great. A planter, writing his name De Boyce, lived in the parish of Saint Michael, Barbadoes, in 1680 ; as a family tradition states that Boyce is a name of Norman extraction, it may be supposed the name was probably written "de Boyce" originally. Names of different members of the families mentioned above, are found on the various public records of the State of North Carolina, showing that they have ever been ready to serve both their country and their state, in times of war and of peace. William Hardy Boyce, and his wife, Mary Eliza (Polly) Harrell, parents of Mrs. Edgar, were children of neighboring planters. Mr. Boyce was born near Windsor, Bertie County, North Carolina, in 1796, and his wife, in the same state and county, two years later. Mr. Boyce's mother having died during his early childhood, his father married a second wife. About the period of 1812, Mr. Boyce lost his father also. Soon after this event, he entered the American army, and remained until the close of the War of 1812. Mary Eliza Harrell was bereft of both parents, when quite an infant, and was committed to the fostering care of an older brother, Mr. Gabriel Harrell ; as a guardian, he remained faithful to his trust, until his little ward grew into womanhood, and finally took upon herself the vows of a wife, on her marriage with William Hardy Boyce, in 1816.

In 1818 Mr. Boyce removed from North Carolina to the State of Alabama, and it was at Huntsville, Alabama, November 5, 1819, that Mary Ann Boyce was born, she being the second daughter, as well as the second child, born into the family. In 1828 Mr. Boyce again changed his place of residence, and arrived at St. Louis, Missouri, November, 1828, accompanied by his wife and three children, two daughters ; i. e., Margaret E. (Mrs. Joseph Rowe, of Missouri), Mary Ann (Mrs. Timothy B. Edgar) and Samuel H., deceased, a little daughter having died in infancy at Huntsville, Alabama. Mr. Boyce soon become a successful lumber merchant, but about the period of 1840–41 he withdrew from this branch of commerce and built several steamers, placing them on the Mississippi and Missouri rivers. Mr. Boyce died at St. Louis, June, 1849, soon after the great fire, at the comparatively early age of fifty-two years and some months.

The year 1849 is a year memorable in the history of St. Louis; a year marked by fire, flood and that dread scourge, cholera. Mr. Boyce was an earnest and devout churchman, of the Episcopalian faith, but as there was no Episcopal church in St. Louis at the period of his arrival in that city, he, with his wife, united with the Methodist Episcopal church, in which connection they remained during the later years of life. Notwithstanding the period at which he lived and the scenes amidst which he dwelt, Mr. Boyce was a man of remarkable Christian character. We mention two facts, associated with his business career, which illustrate the principles and the character of the man, facts which are as pertinent to this day, as they were to the period of which we write. Mr. Boyce allowed no intoxicating liquors to be sold upon his steamers, nor could those traveling under his auspices, engage in any games of chance, where gambling might be introduced — a baneful custom, which haunted steamer traffic, during the early part of this century. Isolated pictures flash upon the dim, far-away childhood-memory of the writer: now, a bright, genial face, on which a wealth of love and kindly feeling are portrayed ; now, a pleasant, melodious voice falls upon the ear, as one, with the presence and carriage of a Southern gentleman of the "old school," appears upon the scene. Again, a child, with arms clasped about the neck of grandpapa ; her young face is pressed closely against that of the older one, while her slight figure is enfolded within strong loving arms. Thus, after the lapse of years, are the happy memories of the hours spent with grandfather vividly recalled by one of his loved ones.

Although Mrs. Boyce survived her husband until the year 1876, the wellspring of life seems to have, in a measure, ceased to flow at his death. Through a long period of widowhood she mourned the loss of loved ones, and in later years the devastation of her beloved Southland by war. Intense in her love, so was she also intense in feeling, concerning every relation in life; yet midst it all she was ever the proud Southern dame, and suffered, as only such natures can suffer, as she witnessed the violent changes that occurred during and after the great Civil War. Mrs. Boyce was deft in the use of her needle, and it gave her great pleasure to present to both children and grandchildren, skillfully-wrought pieces of her handiwork, which have been carefully preserved and are highly prized by her descendants. At the closing years of her long life of nearly eighty years, Mrs. Boyce oftentimes remarked, that the scenes of her life had been so varied and so woven into the early history of the nation, that if she should write of these events, the story would be as interesting and thrilling as any romance ever written. Oh, that we had insisted, that she put such recollections . upon paper! How we would scan the pages now, in this our four-hundredth-anniversary-year! How we should enjoy the quaint pictures of early national life, together with bits of history, which are often preserved, only by those who are closely associated with certain passing events.

CHAPTER III.

A virtuous woman who can find?
For her price is far above rubies.
The heart of her husband trusteth in her,
And he shall have no lack of gain.
She doeth him good and not evil
All the days of her life.——
She girdeth her loins with strength,
And maketh strong her arms.——
Her lamp goeth not out by night.——
She spreadeth out her hand to the poor ;
Yea, she reacheth forth her hands to the needy.
She is not afraid of the snow for her household ;
For all her household are clothed with scarlet.——
Her husband is known in the gates,
When he sitteth among the elders of the land.——
Strength and dignity are her clothing ; ——
She looketh well to the ways of her household,
And eateth not the bread of idleness.
Her children rise up and call her blessed ;
Her husband also.——
A woman that feareth the Lord, she shall be praised.——

—Prov. xxxi.

WE will now return to the year 1828, at which
period Mrs. Edgar, then a child of nine years,
found herself surrounded by new and varied scenes in the
city of St. Louis. She recalls vividly the appearance
of the city during the days of her early girlhood ; the
few narrow streets, the rolling commons and the pleasant
meadow-lands beyond, all of which at this day are occupied by great buildings in the heart of the oldest districts
of the city. The little maiden was all life and action ; she

24

Mrs. Y. B. Edgar

reveled in outdoor life, and as she grew in years, it was her delight to make purchases according to the needs of the household, so far as her youth and judgment would permit. The little shopping excursions met in a great degree, the cravings of her active nature, and gave play to those faculties of her mind, which in after years developed into large executive ability. We must remember, at that day, there were scarcely any of those games for girls which are now found so pleasant and healthful, and yielding much enjoyment to those for whom they are planned. In after years, Mrs. Edgar's children, always greatly enjoyed the stories of "mother's pets when she was a little girl." These pets were many and of various kinds ; to their history her children would listen with bated breath, for strange to say, almost all came to some sad tragic end, bringing sorrow and dismay to the little woman by whom they were so fondly cherished. Thus, early in life, was manifested a warm, loving heart, an inheritance bequeathed to her by both parents. Mrs. Edgar was educated at the St. Louis Institute. This institute was established and conducted by the Misses Stibbs, noted educators in St. Louis in the early part of this century, whose work was largely known and recognized as of marked influence, not only in educational circles, but in the city at large. While under this training Mrs. Edgar developed a taste for music, drawing and painting in water colors. In a specimen of the latter, which has been preserved, we see the same severe and precise type, which is now found in collections of works of art, executed by the maidens of our colonial families of the eighteenth century. At the residence of her parents, August 22, 1837, Mary Ann Boyce gave her hand in marriage to Timothy Bloomfield Edgar. The years sped, and eight children come to gladden their household; two, a son and a daughter, tarried in the earthly home but for a brief space, as the steady stream of united lives swept on, in sunlight and through shadow.

It was not until the Civil War rose as a great tidal wave, threatening to engulf and destroy all things before it, that Mrs. Edgar's decisive character and executive ability were called into action and exercised beyond the precincts of her own home. Though a Southern woman in nature and character, as well as by birth, she had settled in her own mind, the question in its embryo, years before, when the Methodist Episcopal church, of which she was a member, separated, forming a Methodist Episcopal Church South and a Methodist Episcopal Church North. Mrs. Edgar decided she could not walk with either, since, in her mind, the church should know no North, no South, no East, no West, but should constitute one body in the Lord Christ Jesus. Entertaining such principles, she could not accept the Act of Secession in 1861; the union of the States must be preserved, so long as the National Government continued its fostering care ; in union alone was there strength. "United we stand, divided we fall," was her motto. Although at this period, each of her six children, was of an age to require the watchful eye of a mother, yet, when the shock came, and the stern realities of war were felt, she was ready to act in her woman's sphere and to meet the exigencies of the hour. Her watchful eye and guiding hand were not withdrawn in the least from her children or the machinery of her household, neither was hospitality neglected, during the eighteen months, in which she devoted so large a portion of her time and strength to the Nation's welfare. Not, in fact, until the Western Sanitary Commission, the Ladies' Union Aid Society, and the various departments of the National Government, were thoroughly organized and equipped, did she pause in her incessant care for the sick and wounded soldiers, the refugees and the Indians, who were scattered and made destitute by the ravages of war round about them ; and she continued through the entire war, to " lend a hand " in many ways as the occasion required. Mrs. Edgar was one of the few ladies who met at the home of Mrs. F. Holy, July 26, 1861, to discuss ways and means, by which, the efforts of the ladies of St. Louis, who desired to sustain the Federal Government, might be united.

After the severe battles in Missouri, she assisted Mr. James E. Yateman, president of the Western Sanitary Commission, and others, in gathering nurses, buying hospital supplies and getting in readiness the new House of Refuge Hospital, to which hospital, the first hundred of the sick and wounded were taken. At this time, "there was no room in the hospitals, no clothing, no stores of food and medicines, no surgical corps, no preparation in any department." A call was issued by Gen. John C. Frémont, Commandant of the Department of the West, for lint, bandages, etc., and for ladies to assist in preparing them ; an apartment was assigned for the reception of these articles at General Frémont's headquarters. In the course of a few weeks the room was needed for other purposes, and then it was, that Mrs. Edgar offered to have these hospital stores removed to her own home, situated on the same avenue, not many blocks distant from General Frémont's residence. Two large apartments in her house were set apart to receive them, and here, for eighteen months, women wrought. Lint, bandages and hospital clothing were made, stores and garments were received, and sent to various points, where battles raged, and where the wounded and sick lay in temporary hospitals. All articles and moneys received, were duly recorded by Mrs. Edgar's secretary, together with the donors, as well as the points to which the stores were sent.

It was during these months, that Mrs. Edgar was greatly assisted by many German ladies of the city, women of culture, of "gentle blood" and of marked refinement, in character and disposition. They seemed to know instinctively, woman's work and place, midst war and conflict. Alas! in their native land, the clash of arms, the moving of great armies, had been seen and heard, and with womanly grace, they had stood and ministered to the suffering ones, who dropped by the wayside as the conflict rolled on. Their kindly aid was gratefully accepted by our American women, who were stunned and appalled for the moment, when suddenly they found themselves face to face with the stern realities of war. In order to facilitate the work, Mrs. Edgar organized her assistants, calling the organization the Frémont Relief Society, as it was in answer to an appeal of General Frémont, that this branch of work had its origin. Several times Mrs. Edgar, accompanied by a co-worker, visited hospital camps in various parts of the State, to note what was needed and to see that certain supplies were promptly delivered. Of the Mississippi Valley Sanitary Fair, held at St. Louis, May, 1864 (the object of which was to raise a fund for the sick and wounded of the armies of the Mississippi Valley, under the general direction of the Western Sanitary Commission), Mrs. Edgar was a member of the Executive Committee of Ladies, and was chairman of a Linen Department, which netted to the Fair the sum of two thousand three hundred and ninety-six dollars.

After the close of the Civil War, Mrs. Edgar greatly enjoyed her European tour with her husband and several members of her family. An older daughter, recalls the lively description her mother gave of her travels, soon after her return, as she turned from one view to another, the views being systematically arranged according to the plan of her journeyings. So vivid was the impression made, that in later years, after hearing one of the popular "Stoddard Lectures," the daughter remarked to her husband, "that neither the views, nor the descriptions, were quite equal, to the little illustrated talk her mother gave one morning, soon after her European tour." On the certificate of incorporation of the St. Louis Woman's Christian Association, organized December, 1868, stands the name of "Mary A. Edgar," and of which body her name appears as vice-president. For a number of years Mrs. Edgar was also a member of the Board of Managers of the St. Louis Protestant Orphan Asylum. She was elected to the office of vice-president of the same institution, but resigned after a brief term, as other matters claimed her time and attention.

The sentiments that have been expressed in prose, poetry and song, extolling a mother's love and devotion, are beautifully illustrated in Mrs. Edgar's character as a mother ; and now, as she enjoys with her husband the quiet of their delightful home, she looks out upon the surging world with interest, but cares not to mingle with its strife and bustle ; for has she not, even as her husband, served her generation ? And her children, engaged and interested in the intense life of great cities, as they pass to and from the parental home, arise, as the children of old, and call her blessed.

TO OUR DEAR PARENTS ON THEIR GOLDEN WEDDING DAY.

AUGUST 22, 1887.

I.

Father, mother dear,
Far away by the dark blue sea,
Where every whispering zephyr,
Every passing breeze,
Every dash of the briny spray,
Every song of the murmuring wave,
Bring to you by their fairy touch,
A priceless gift, not glittering gold,
But the gift of health, the strength of old.

II.

The Golden Day has come,
The cycle is complete,
We would not call you home,
To the city's heated halls,
To its parched and arid streets,
At this, our festive hour.
What more fitting, than to keep
This golden tide by the sea,

To celebrate at dear Old Rye
The Golden Wedding Day.
Where, in deep glades of fragrant pine,
'Mid skies of blue and fields of green,
Lulled by the music of the waves,
So many peaceful days have sped.

III.

After a voyage of fifty years
O'er rolling billows and summer seas,
Through threatening storms and wintry blasts,
Could there be a fairer haven,
In which to tarry, and celebrate,
This happy, joyful, Wedding Day?

IV.

To us, no parents e'er like ours,
None, so good and true,
As down through all the golden years
Chime the sweet memories,
Of fond parental love.

V.

And now, sweet bells, o'er land and sea,
Ring out, ring out, a joyful peal
On this the Golden Nuptial Day.

VI.

At this eventful tide, we children six,
To our parental shrine, no worldly treasures bring ;
No pearls from the silent deep,
No gems from Afric's burning sands,
But, enshrined, within a circle, veiled to human
    sight,
We bring, six living, loving, loyal, hearts.
Ye know them well, we need not speak,
For midst the peal of wedding bells,
We humbly lay them at your feet.

VII.

Before Him, who with tender care
Hath kept you, through all the changing years,
We sound our grateful hallelujahs.
May the incense of loving hearts,
Swell the anthem sweet and clear,
As we pray, that o'er your pathway
Golden blessings e'er may shower,
Bathing the landscape, in effulgence bright,
Till it reaches, afar, the eternal heights.

F. H. E. R.

TO OUR DEAR FATHER, ON HIS SEVENTY-FIFTH BIRTHDAY.

JANUARY 20TH, 1890.

I.

Dear father, we come with a greeting to you,
Bearing garlands fresh as the morning dew,
Wreathed into crowns of a sparkling hue,
We greet the new year with this tribute to you.

II.

But the day that we hail and so happily note,
The anniversary day of your birth,
We greet with songs of gladsome mirth ;
'Tis the day that brings to us more joy,
Than any bright hope of sunny cheer
Wafted to us by the glad new year.

III.

In songs of praise our hearts we raise
Through many hopes and fears,
For life and health vouchsafed to you
These five and seventy years.

Changing years, of varied hue,
Studded with blessings not a few,
'Mid skies of soft ethereal blue,
These years have brought good gifts to you.

IV.

How thankful we are for your fireside bright,
Where the world doth not enter its comfort to blight.
Here the children still gather, in sorrow and joy,
And in its soft, radiant light, many hours employ
In recalling sweet memories, only time can destroy.

V.

Dear father, now we bid you adieu,
With the loving wish, that both mother and you,
Continue to welcome, as your hearts' delight,
Both children and friends, to your fireside bright.

VI.

When, in future years to come,
We are gathered, one by one,
To our blessed home above,
May ours be, an unbroken band,
Redeemed, made perfect, by the blood of the Lamb.

F. H. E. R.

JAMES EDGAR

APPENDIX.

Of the different Saxon families that became identified with the Scottish nation, at the period of the Norman Conquest, some are more prominent than others. The history of the well-known line of Edgar Etheling or Atheling, the fourth remove from Ethelred II, and the heir to the Saxon line of kings, as well as that of his sister, the Princess Margaret, afterward, as the wife of Malcolm III of Scotland, the Scottish queen, so greatly beloved by king and people, is familiar to all ; but not so, perhaps, is that of the Saxon-Scottish House of Dunbar. An ancestress of this house was the Princess Elgiva, daughter of Ethelred II, King of the Anglo-Saxons, and granddaughter of Edgar, the Saxon King of England, and the wife of Uchtred,* Prince of Northumbria, England. Their daughter and heiress, Algetha, written also Algitha, was given in marriage to Maldred, grandson of Malcolm II of Scotland, and brother to the "gracious King Duncan" of the same country. The first Gospartick, or Cospatrick, Earl of Northumbria, son of Maldred and Algitha, was

---

* Siward, the Giant Earl of Northumberland, is stated to have married Aelfled, the great-granddaughter of Waltheof. Waltheof, born about A. D. 969, was the father of Uchtred.

confirmed in the earldom of Northumbria by William the
Conqueror in 1067. He (Cospatrick) received a grant of
Dunbar, Scotland, with the lands in Lothian, from his
kinsman, Malcolm III, in 1072, probably a portion of
the same territory wrested from his ancestors by Malcolm
II in 1018.

The following bit of history, gleaned from "Genealog-
ical Collections Concerning the Scottish House of Edgar," * with occasional notes and remarks added by
the compiler,† may be of interest to the descendants of
that ancient house. The second Cospatrick of Northumbria, or Northumberland, England, was the first
Earl of Dunbar, and the fourth Cospatrick, the third
Earl of Dunbar ; Edgar, third son of the third Earl
of Dunbar (period of time, about the middle of the
twelfth century), appears to have been ancestor of
those of the surname Edgar.‡ A charter is vouched
of Earl Patrick, son of Waldeve, Earl of Dunbar, who
grants to the monks of Durham the church and lands of
Edram for prayers to be said * * etc. The charter
is granted in the reign of King William of Scotland,

* Grampian Club, London, 1873.

† F. H. E. R., 1892.

‡ " Verstigan derives the name from Ead, an oath, and —— to keep."
Webster's International Dictionary : a javelin (or protector) of property.

and contains many witnesses, and among them appears the name of Willielm, filius Edgari. This William, son of Edgar, seems to have been one of the progenitors of Edgar of Wadderlie (period of time, probably toward the close of the twelfth century). ("The principal family of the name of Edgar there, is Edgar of Wadderlie, yet extant, who carried for their proper arms — Sable, a lion rampant argent." As the arms of the House of Wedderlie are found in armorial sculpture among its ancient ruins, they were probably adopted at an early period and made permanent during the reign of King William of Scotland (1165) "when armorial bearings were first assumed by warriors and men of consequence.") The territory, once in the possession of the Wadderlie, or Wedderlie family, appears to have extended in a broken chain, from the coast of Berwickshire, Scotland, to the Solway Firth. Descriptions are given in various grants and deeds of the lands, in which are mentioned the tower, fortalice and manor houses of Wedderlie, the buildings, gardens, mills, mill lands, multures, meadows, pastures, parts, pendicles and pertinents of its towns and parishes.

Toward the close of the thirteenth century, an Edgar, Laird of Wedderlie (probably Sir Patrick Edgar, Knt.), appears to have married a Countess of Home.* Early in the following century, during the reign of King Robert

---

* The House of Home, a cadet of the House of Dunbar.

the Bruce, at whose marriage Richard de Edgar* was a witness ; the House of Wedderlie seems to have reached the summit of its prosperity. Richard de Edgar, in the reign of King Robert the Bruce, married the eldest daughter and co-heiress of Ros of Sanquhar,† and William de Crichton or Crechton (ancestor of the Earl of Dumfries) married a younger daughter. During the reign of the Bruce, the barony was divided between Richard Edgar and William Crichton and Isabella, his wife. King Robert confirmed to Richard de Edgar and his son, the castle and half the barony of Sanquhar, in Upper Nithsdale,‡ also Dumfries and the lands of Ellioc, as well as those of Bartmonade and of Lobri, of Slochan, of Glenabenkan, and part of the lands of Kirkpatrick. Of the same king, Richard also obtained the barony of Kirkandrews, Wigtoun.

One of Richard's four sons (Donald Edgar), was placed at the head of the Clan MacGowan in Nithsdale, by King David II of Scotland, while the older brother (Richard), seems to have resigned Wedderlie to a younger brother, Robert Edgar Dominus de Wedderlie, who was probably a godson of King Robert the Bruce.

---

* Unlike the majority of noble surnames, this is not territorial ; twice only in the ancient records, which have escaped the hand of the destroyer, is an Edgar named William de Wedderlie.

† The barony of Sanquhar, situated in Southern Scotland, comprised a portion, if not all, of the present county of Dumfries.

‡ Nithsdale, located in the same county (Dumfries), is traversed by the river Nith.

It is probable, that in the fourteenth century, the House of Wedderlie was more powerfully represented in Nithsdale than in its native shire (Berwick). The Laird of Wedderlie, as co-representative of Robert de Ros,* Lord of Sanquhar, through his wife, a daughter of the latter, was allied to the family of one of the competitors for the Crown of Scotland in 1292, thus his position must have been among the foremost in the kingdom.

Yet it seems strange, that when a distinction came gradually to be made between territorial and titular barons, an Edgar should have acquired the latter rank ; thus losing for his descendants a nominal status, which, like many powerful barons, they perhaps undervalued during the season of material prosperity, and before the encroachments of men, inferior by birth, but more ambitious — had reduced, by taking advantage of their inaptitude for war or business, or by marriage with their daughters, the once noble possessions of the family to comparatively a few acres.† Moreover, they were among the few families who disobeyed the Act of 1672, in not having their arms matriculated in the Lyon Register then established. Then again, the direct succession seems to have been more than once broken, and though it is incontro-

*William de Ros, great-grandson of Isabella, said to have been eldest daughter of King William of Scotland.

† The ancient manor house, once styled a fortalice, and about six thousand acres, chiefly moorland, picturesquely extending toward the Lammermoor Hills, are all that now represent the lordly possessions of this once powerful family.

vertible, that even during the most troublous times, Wedderlie was never held but by an Edgar, still, at the period mentioned (1672), the Laird of Wedderlie may have been self-sufficient and short-sighted, or ignorant of the intention of the act referred to, and content to thus proceed on the principle of "leaving well enough alone." The lands of Wedderlie continued in the possession of the Edgar family until 1733-6, when they passed by sale to Robert Lord Blantyre. An apocryphal story is told of the departure of the Edgars of Wedderlie, from their ancient inheritance, the family being obliged to sell the estates ; and, in the words of the narrator, " the auld laird and leddy drove out in their carriage and four horses at midday ; but the young laird (their only child), was broken-hearted at the thocht o' leaving the auld place, and he waited till the darkening ; for he said, the sun should na shine when he left his hame." The preserver of this anecdote was a very aged woman, named Eppy Forsyth, who died about 1840. She remembered seeing the young laird riding down the avenue alone, and she said, " It was a dark nicht when the last Edgar rode out of Wedderlie."*

In the " Bride of Lammermoor," there are a few

* Rear-Admiral Alexander Edgar, who died at London, England, March, 1817, at the age of eighty years, was the last male descendant (so far as known) of the ancient Scottish family of Edgar of Wedderlie. The last Laird of Wedderlie had five sons, of whom the Admiral was one ; it seems remarkable, that none of them should have left any known male descendants.

marked and curious coincidences, between the family of Ravenswood and that of Edgar of Wedderlie. Both were of the Merse, and Wedderlie is situated at the foot of the Lammermoor Hills ; the Master of Ravenswood is named Edgar. Against the " Wolf's Crag " of the Romance, we have " Wolfstruther," afterward Westruther, the parish of Wedderlie. Edgar Ravenswood was related to the Humes and Douglases ; so likewise was Edgar of Wedderlie ; but what is still more remarkable, both families were connected with that of Chiesly, and at the same period. The Ravenswoods were involved in a litigation in which Chiesly was implicated ; while in the public records at the period of the Romance, Edgar of Wedderly had a bitter lawsuit with Chiesly, the tutor of his father's younger children. Edgar of Wedderly was impoverished by his opposition to the Presbyterian Church, just as Edgar Ravenswood opposed its minister at his father's funeral. Both families were turbulent, and both were brought to ruin by espousing the losing cause.

The House of Keithock,* a cadet of the House of

* The estate of Kethick, or Keithock, a portion of the ancient possessions of the noble House of Lindsay, situated in Forfarshire, on the Eastern coast of Scotland (the Firth of Tay forming a part of its southern boundary), came into the Edgar family early in the seventeenth century. The name Edgar is found in the locality at an early period ; from 1202 to 1218, when the signatures of Robert and Thomas Edgar were attached to charters of the Bishop of Brechin, in favor of the abbey of Arbroath. In old registers, the barony of Keithock is described in a similar manner, as that of Wedderlie. The manor place and mansion house, including the town and lands of Laidsyd, the town and lands of Builbuttis are mentioned, with the tenants, and services of free tenants ; also houses, gardens, orchards, woods, fishings, moors, crofts, etc., all lying within the regality of Brechin, barony of Keithock, and sheriffdom of Forfar.

Wedderlie, was established in the seventeenth century. Several members of this house were devotedly attached to the House of Stewart, though they themselves were adherents to the Episcopal faith. John and James, sons of David Edgar, of Keithock, were prominent in the Rebellion of 1715. The former died a prisoner in Stirling Castle, and the latter, escaping to Italy, became private secretary to the Chevalier de Saint George, termed by the Scots, King James VIII; and occupied this post for the long period of fifty years. He was one of the few Scottish gentlemen, who formed the small court of the Chevalier, and shared with him, the long, weary years of exile. During his exile in Rome, Secretary Edgar appears to have been in straightened circumstances, due, in a great measure, to his scruples, which, as a Protestant, incapacitated him from holding such remunerative positions under the Pontifical Government, as the Chevalier might otherwise have obtained for him. The British Government, having reason to believe, that another attempt for the restoration of the exiled family was about to be made, Sir Robert Walpole,* Prime Minister of England, discovered through intrigue, the great confidence reposed by the Chevalier in his private secretary, and offered a handsome sum to the latter to induce him to betray

* Of whom Sir Walter Scott writes: "Disbelieving in the very existence of patriotism, he (Sir Robert Walpole) held the opinion, that every man had his price, and might be bought, if his services were worth the value at which he rated them."—" Tales of a Grandfather."

the intention of the Prince. But the secretary, indignantly put the letter in the fire and returned no answer.

Several other offers, gradually increasing in amount, followed, but met with the same fate; until at length, Sir Robert, imagining that he had not yet come up to the secretary's price, wrote to the latter, informing him that £10,000 had been placed to his credit in the Bank of Venice; whereupon the secretary consulted the Chevalier, and after a brief interval replied; and while thanking Sir Robert for the money (which he had lost no time in drawing from the bank), informed him, that he had just "laid it at the feet of his royal master, who had the best title to gold that came, as this had, from *his own* dominions." The Chevalier was deeply moved by this unexpected service, and in token of his gratitude, presented to his faithful adherent a valuable souvenir, which has been preserved by his representatives, and is now in the possession of James David Edgar, Esq., •of Toronto, head of the House of Keithock. Another member of the House of Keithock, John Edgar, a nephew of the Secretary, united his fortune with that of Prince Charles Edward Stewart. After the decisive battle of Culloden, he arrived, a fugitive, at Keithock, and by a curious coincidence, sought the protection and aid of the same farmer, who, thirty years before, had facilitated the escape of his uncle. To his surprise, he was told that he should be accommodated with the identical clothes in which his relative had found safety. After many unsuccessful attempts, the fugitive gave up the idea of escaping to the Continent, as all the ports were strictly watched. He therefore determined on joining his uncle Thomas, whose home had been in New Jersey for several years, and accordingly, without difficulty, embarked for America. After a week of perilous delay on the coast of Scotland, the skipper continued the voyage; but they were scarcely halfway across the Atlantic when they were chased by a French privateer. Anxiously as everyone else on board hoped to escape, the fugitive Jacobite had other thoughts ; and when they were ultimately captured, on discovering himself to his captors, his property was restored. On being carried into a French port, he proceeded at once to Paris, where he obtained a commission in Lord Ogilvy's regiment of the Scottish Brigade. Afterward he joined his uncle (the Secretary), at Rome ; and in 1756, after the publication of the Act of Indemnity, returned to Scotland. The following anecdote is related of Mr. John Edgar and Prince Charles Edward. The former was Postmaster-General to the Prince during his brief occupation of Edinburgh. One of his duties was to examine all letters leaving the town. In a letter from a young lady to a friend in the country, she mentioned that the rebels were in the town 1,000 strong. This being nearly the truth, Mr. Edgar asked the Prince whether the letter might be forwarded ; '' add a ' o,' '' was his reply, and " let it go." Cardinal York appreciated the services of the Edgars, and in the family of the latter, are many of the personal effects of the father and mother of the Cardinal, besides other valuable relics of the Stewart family, the bequests of the Cardinal to Mr. Edgar.* Secretary Edgar's eldest brother, Alexander, succeeded to the estate of Keithock ; a younger brother, Henry, was third and last Bishop of Fife.

Secretary James Edgar, eighth son of David Edgar, Laird of Keithock, died in exile September 24, 1764 (unmarried). His nephew John, who succeeded to the estate of Keithock,† survived him until the year 1788, when he expired, soon after receiving the tidings of the death of Prince Charles Edward. One member of the family meets a lonely death at Stirling Castle, another dies in exile far from home and kindred, and in the third, the sands of life, silently ebb, when those of his beloved prince cease to flow. Surely, faithful unto death, were these three cavaliers of Keithock, in their devotion to the House of Stewart. Thomas,‡ fifth son of David Edgar, of Keithock, proceeded to America in 1725, and there pur-

---

* These relics are still (1892) in the possession of the Edgar family, Toronto, Canada.

† Keithock passed out of the possession of the Edgar family in 1790, two years after the death of John Edgar, the Secretary's nephew. James David Edgar, the fourth in descent from John Edgar, the last Laird of Keithock, is a barrister-at-law, at Toronto, and Member of the Canadian Parliament. He is head, and the present, (1892), representative of the House of Keithock.

‡ Ancestor of Timothy Bloomfield Edgar, St. Louis, Missouri, U. S. A.

chased an estate near the city of Elizabeth, State of New Jersey, which he styled Edgarton, after his family name. The estate continued in the Edgar family until the year 1885. Of his numerous descendants, many have held influential positions, in the various states of the Union. In each generation, members of the family have stood ready, to assist the new nation in its hour of need — in the War of Independence, in the War of 1812, as well as in the great Civil War. May the noble and ancient name of Edgar, ever continue to be a bulwark of the American Nation, so long as the Nation's name is a synonym for righteousness, truth, freedom and honor.

www.ingramcontent.com/pod-product-compliance
Lightning Source LLC
Chambersburg PA
CBHW021231260626
47172CB00002B/715